To: Elizabeth

From: Uncle Mike & Aunt Paula

1/93.

minnie 'n me

BLUE-RIBBON FRIENDS

BY Lyn Calder

ILLUSTRATED BY Vaccaro Associates

DISNEY PRESS

NEW YORK

Minnie 'n Me: Blue-Ribbon Friends
is published by Disney Press,
a subsidiary of The Walt Disney Company,
500 South Buena Vista Street,
Burbank, California 91521.
The story and art herein are copyright © 1991
The Walt Disney Company.
No part of this book may be printed
or reproduced in any manner whatsoever,
whether mechanical or electronic,
without the written permission of the publisher.
The stories, characters or incidents
in this publication are entirely fictional.

Published by Disney Press
114 Fifth Avenue
New York, New York 10011

Printed in the U.S.A.
ISBN 1-56282-034-6
8 7 6 5 4 3 2 1

This book is dedicated to

Paste your
photo here

"My grandma sent me the new 'Climb the Ladder' game," said Minnie. "Who wants to play?"

"I do!" said Penny.

"Me, too," said Daisy. "I saw some kids playing at
school. It looked like fun."

Minnie spun the dial to see who would go first.
The dial pointed to Daisy.

"Oh, goody!" said Daisy. "I'm first."

Penny spun the dial next. This time it pointed to Minnie.

"Oh, boo," said Penny. "That means I'm last."

Daisy started the game. She picked up a card and read it out loud: "Hop on your right foot four times. Turn around twice. Then move three rungs up the ladder."

"This is going to be fun!" said Daisy. She did four hops, made two turns, and then moved her marker three rungs up the ladder.

Next it was Minnie's turn. She picked a card and
read it: "You look tired. Do not move up any rungs."
Now it was Minnie's turn to say, "Oh, boo!"

Penny picked the next card. It said: "Shake each player's hand. Then move six rungs up the ladder." "Six rungs! Hurray!" said Penny.

Minnie, Daisy, and Penny took turns picking cards
and doing the funny things the cards told them to do.
Minnie had to sing her favorite song while jumping
up and down.

Daisy had to think of three words that rhymed with "bunny."

And Penny had to say and spell her name backwards.

Finally Penny called out, "I won! I won! I'm the first one up the ladder."

Minnie was only two steps away from the top. But Daisy was all the way down near the bottom.

"I don't like this game," said Daisy in a huff. She stomped off to sit in a corner and mope.

"You're being a sore loser," said Penny.

"Why don't we all play word bingo?" asked Minnie.

"I don't want to. I don't want to lose again," said Daisy. She stayed right where she was.

So Minnie and Penny played word bingo without Daisy. Penny picked a card and read it out loud. The word was "cow."

"I've got 'cow' on my bingo board!" said Penny.
"I've got it, too!" said Minnie.
They each covered the word with their markers.
Minnie picked the next card. The word was "shoe."
Minnie had it on her board. Penny didn't.

They went back and forth picking cards and
covering boxes. Then Minnie jumped up and
shouted, "Bingo! I won!"

Penny stomped her foot. "That means I lost," she
said. "I don't want to play anymore."

"Now who's being a sore loser?" said Minnie.
"I don't care," said Penny. She marched off to sit
in the corner opposite Daisy.

Minnie was left to play all by herself. But she did not want to play alone.

"Some friends you are," said Minnie to Daisy and Penny. She stomped her foot and sat down by her bed.

"Sitting here doing nothing is no fun at all," thought Minnie. So she took her box of dress-up clothes out from under the bed.

Right on top was a pair of blue high-heeled shoes. Minnie put them on. Then she pulled out a long string of shiny pearls.

Minnie got up to look at herself in the mirror. She
twirled around once. She twirled around twice.
"Don't I look wonderful!" she said.

Daisy looked at Minnie. Penny looked at Minnie, too. "What a beautiful boa," said Minnie, as she waved it in the air.

Daisy couldn't sit still any longer. She jumped up.
"Can I wear that?" she asked.

"I don't think it would look good on a sore loser,"
said Minnie.

"I'm finished being a sore loser," said Daisy. She
took the boa and threw it around her shoulders.

"I'm finished being a sore loser, too," said Penny, taking out a bright red cape with sequins. "But if you lost, Minnie, you wouldn't like it either."

Minnie thought about that. "You're right," she
said. "This is what I think we should do. We should
promise that we will be sore losers for only one
minute. Then we have to do something else."

"Good idea," said Penny. "Everyone hold up your
right hand and say 'I promise.' "

"I promise!" said the three friends.

Soon Minnie, Daisy, and Penny were all dressed up like movie stars.

They took turns dancing and singing. Then they
lined up and kicked their legs high in the air.

Minnie took three blue ribbons out of her box of dress-up clothes.

"Here's a ribbon for you, Daisy. Here's one for you, Penny. And here's one for me," she said. "That's because when it comes to being friends, nobody loses, and...

"Everybody wins!"